The Hero of Bremen

retold by MARGARET HODGES

with illustrations by
CHARLES MIKOLAYCAK

Holiday House / New York

The motto on the shield of Roland reads as follows in "Niederdeutsch," a northern German dialect:

vryheit do.ik.yu openbar.de karl
und menich vorst vorwar
desser.stede.ghegheuen.hat.
des.danket.gode.is my radt

in modern German:

freiheit tu ich euch offenbaren.die karl
und mancher fürst fürwahr
dieser stätte gegeben hat
das danket gott ist mein rat

in English:

I reveal to you the freedom which Karl
And many a prince indeed
Have bestowed upon this place.
You'd be wise to thank God for this deed.

The Hero of Bremen

For Fletcher—
a good tale to shorten a journey M.H.

The race is not to the swift . . . *Ecclesiastes* 9: 11

To Anna-Lido, for later C.M.

Author's Note

THE HERO OF BREMEN is based on a legend that was retold in *Bremen's Volkssagen* herausgegeben von Friedrich Wagenfeld : Bremen. Verlag von Wilh. Kaiser, 1845. This German text was sent to me by the librarian of the Staats- und Universitätsbibliothek in Bremen. A graduate assistant in the German department at the University of Pittsburgh translated another version for me. She is married to a German from Bremen. He says, incidentally, that during World War II, when Bremen was bombed, an American pilot spared the old marketplace.

A beautiful and much longer version of the story, "The Frog of Roland," was told in English by Margery Bailey in her collection, *Whistle for Good Fortune,* published by Little, Brown and Company in 1940. At the end of Margery Bailey's tale, the cobbler dies. In the two German versions that I have read—there may be others—he is rewarded and lives happily ever after. To Margery Bailey, I owe the detail that Hans was the name of the hero and that he was a shoemaker. The German versions that I have read do not give him a name. One calls him simply a cripple, the other, a beggar.

Margaret Hodges

IN THE OLD WALLED CITY OF Bremen there once lived a poor shoemaker named Hans. He lived in a tiny cellar with only one window, and the feet of passersby were his view of the world. His own feet were of little use to him, his legs being too short and weak for walking. But his arms were long and strong, and from hard use his knuckles and knees were tough as a horse's hooves. When he left his cellar to buy bread and cheese for dinner or leather for mending shoes, he went on knuckles and knees, dragging his legs behind him, but he was a cheerful, friendly fellow. As other men's feet passed him in the street, he often felt a pat on his head or heard a voice above him say, "Greetings, Hans Cobbler! How goes it?"

"Never better," he would answer.

Now the south side of Bremen lay along a river where many ships put in to trade, and the townsfolk were so hard-working and thrifty that the city had grown and grown until there was hardly room in which to turn around. Every house was crammed to bursting, from attic to cellar. People elbowed each other in the narrow streets. Children had no room to run and play. There was no pasture for horses or cattle. At last the people agreed to pay a tax for each window in their houses so that Bremen could buy land outside its walls. Even Hans paid the tax for his little window.

Hans's pockets were more often empty than full, though he worked from sunup to sundown. He would not hurry his work, finding where a shoe pinched or mending soles so well that he spent an hour doing what other cobblers did with a rat-a-tat-tat in a minute. He stopped work only when children came down the steps of his cellar to hear him tell stories of heroes from times gone by, tall handsome men who could swing into the saddle and ride to battle with banners flying.

Hans loved best the stories about Roland, the famous knight whose uncle, the emperor Charlemagne, had made Bremen a free city. Roland was the hero of Bremen. Hans Cobbler told how Roland won his magic sword and his wonderful ivory horn from a giant, how he led the army of Charlemagne in battle, and died fighting bravely to the last. When he told the old tales, Hans would gaze up through the bars of his little window as if he saw the hooves of Roland's white horse galloping by or heard the sound of an ivory horn blown far away in the woods outside the city walls. The children too looked and listened, for Hans said that Roland would come again in time of need.

But now Bremen did not need a champion to fight battles. It needed room to grow, and Roland did not come to help. The mayor and the city council met and talked the matter over.

"We have raised enough money from our window tax to buy some land," said the mayor. "Let us ask the Countess Emma to meet with us and strike a bargain."

The Countess Emma was a rich and powerful old lady who owned all of the land around Bremen. She lived in a high-towered castle, alone except for her servants and her nephew. He would have all her land and the castle too when she died, and he hoped he would not have long to wait. He was not much pleased when the mayor and the city council asked the countess to meet with them in the marketplace and arrange for a sale of land.

WESER FL
BREMA

On the day of the meeting, all the people of Bremen gathered in the marketplace. Hans worked his way through the crowd to see the table where the money lay tied up in bags. On one side stood the mayor and the city council with the people behind them. At last the countess arrived, carried in a litter. Her nephew rode on horseback at her side, straight and stiff as a poker.

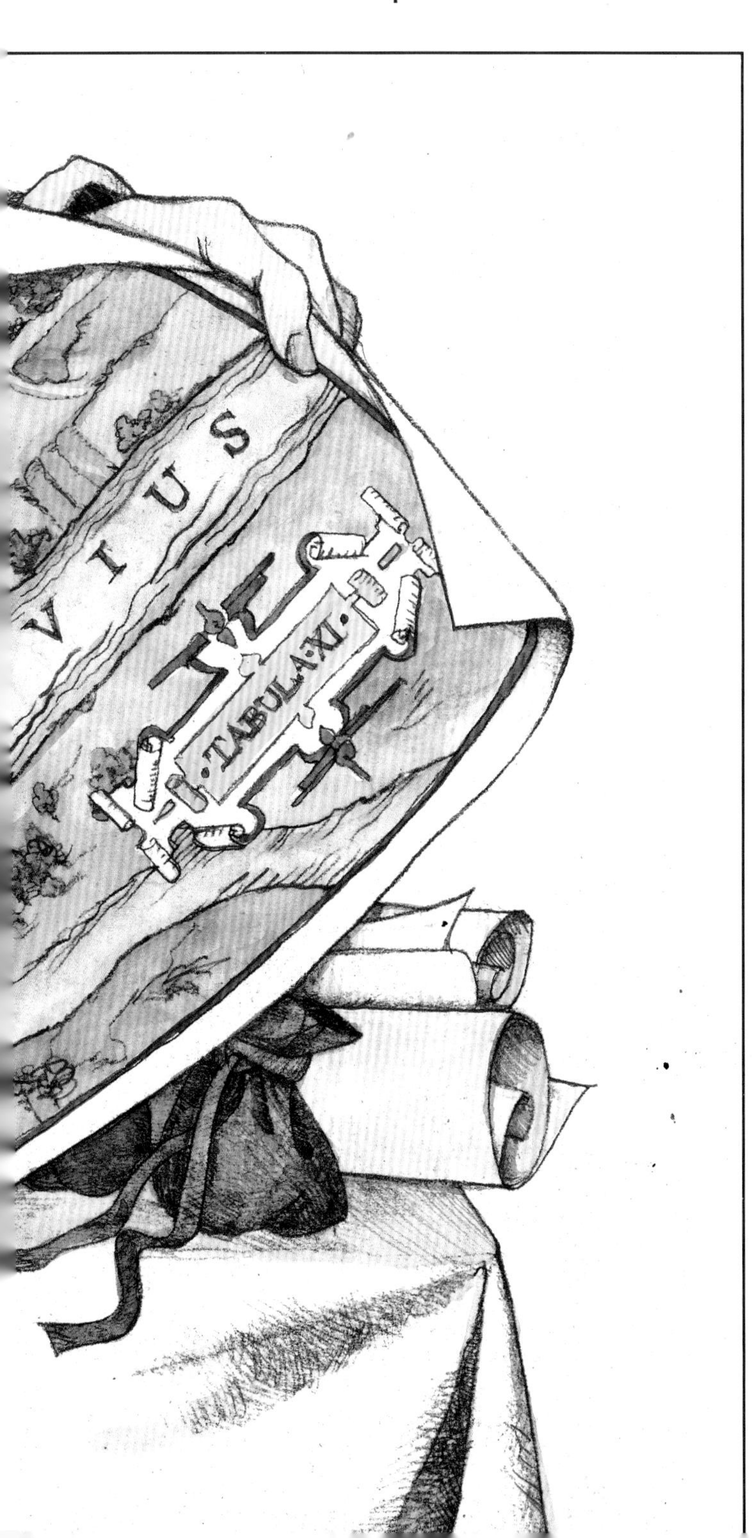

They sat at the table, and the bargaining began. The countess offered this much land for that much money. Too much, not enough, back and forth went the talk between the countess and the mayor, while the nephew said never a word, but stared long and hard at the crowd. At last he spoke.

"Let us cut the matter short. I suggest that my aunt give you good people all the land that a man can walk around in a day. He shall leave the east gate at dawn and enter the west gate before the sun goes down. Would this content you? A free gift, mind you!"

The mayor smiled, the crowd cheered, and the countess patted her nephew's hand, saying, "I am glad to find you so generous, nephew. It shall be as you say. I will reward you for bringing this business to a happy end."

"I ask only one reward," he answered.

"Name it," said she.

"Let me choose the man who will walk around Bremen," said he.

"That is little to ask," she said. "You shall have your wish."

Again he stared into the crowd. Then, smiling into his beard, he pointed at Hans the cobbler and said, "I choose this one."

The mayor's smile faded. The crowd, bitterly disappointed, murmured and mumbled, then fell silent and returned to their homes. They had been tricked, and well tricked. Nothing would change for Bremen.

Hans was dumbfounded. "Nevertheless, I must try," he said, and off he went to his cellar.

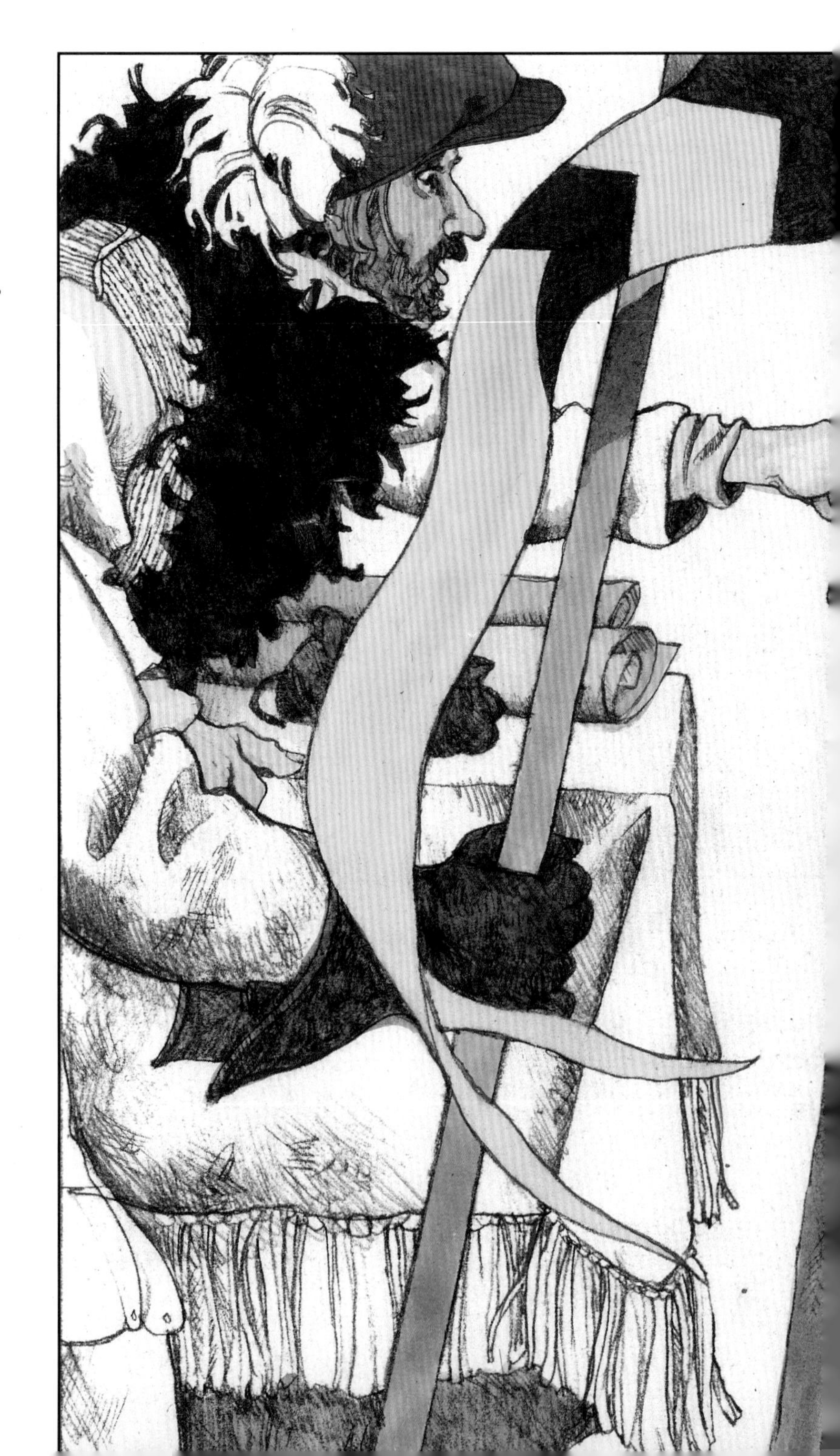

He set to work with all his might, mending every shoe he had left unfinished on his bench, and putting all his tools in order. By dawn, he was at the east gate of the city.

With him came a city councillor to see that all was done fairly. No one else wanted to see such a pitiful sight, except the children, who came for friendship's sake. Three servants of the countess waited at the gate, carrying bags of wooden stakes to mark out the path of Hans Cobbler. He set off at once.

The land around Bremen was part pasture, part bog, and part forest. Even the pasture was hard going for Hans as he crawled forward, knuckles and knees, knuckles and knees, over humps and into hollows, through bramble and brier. He went northward, following his nose, while the sun climbed and climbed in the eastern sky. The children went to play in the pasture and the countess's servants sat down to rest, catching up with Hans from time to time, and driving in their wooden stakes along his path.

"He will not last long," they said. "This will be an easy day's work." When the sun was high in the sky, they had a drink and lay down in the shade of a tree to sleep.

Noontime came, and Hans was still hard at it, knuckles and knees, knuckles and knees, through the pasture. The sun beat down on his back.

"It is hopeless," said the councillor, and he rode back to town. The children went home for their midday dinner, all but one little girl who had an apple in her apron pocket.

"Have a bite," she said. Hans would not. He came to the end of the pastureland and turned westward into the bog.

"You could go around the bog," said the little girl, and ran off to find a way.

But Hans could not wait. Beyond the bog lay the forest. He must cross that too, and the sun was already low in the western sky. He went straight into the bog, pulling himself through water and mud by grasping the low branches of dead trees and watching for hummocks of grass that might hold his weight. But slower and slower he went, and deeper and deeper he sank into mire and mud until at last he lay still, unable to move. He closed his eyes.

"I have failed," he said to himself. "I have failed Bremen."

It was then that he heard a sound. It came from a distance, somewhere in the depths of the forest. Hans opened his eyes and found himself lying under a tree, where he had certainly not been before. Beside him he saw the hooves of a white horse, and, looking up, he knew the rider at once.

He was a knight. Under a flowing cloak he was clad in bright armor with a shield slung over his shoulder. He bore a long sword in a scabbard girded around his waist, and a great ivory horn hung from his saddle. His head was bare.

"It seems that you need help," he said cheerfully. "Let me take you where you are going."

"Sir," said Hans in a daze, "I know who you are, and I thank you, but to ride is not part of my bargain."

"Then I will walk with you," said the knight, and he leaped from his horse.

"This is hardly fitting," said Hans. "I am only a shoemaker, and you are Roland, who did battle for the great Charlemagne and won us our freedom. You are the hero of Bremen."

"Heroes come in all shapes and sizes, and there are many kinds of battle," answered Roland. "I know a hero when I see one. Let us be on our way and see what we can do together."

The sun stood still while they went on side by side, talking of heroes and of battles fought long ago.

The Countess Emma's servants woke up from their naps and scrambled to follow the path that Hans had made, knuckles and knees. How could a lame man have traveled so far and so fast? They did not understand, but they had to believe their eyes, and they drove in their stakes for dear life. The little girl caught up with Hans in sight of the west gate of Bremen, but her eyes were dazzled by the light of the setting sun, and she did not see Roland. She saw only Hans the shoemaker, surrounded by brightness, as she ran ahead to tell the news of his coming.

Hans reached the west gate just at sundown, and found all of Bremen gathered there to meet him. There had not been such rejoicing since the raising of Bremen's walls. The people carried Hans into the square on their shoulders. They gave him a meal the like of which he had never eaten, and they honored him for the rest of his life.

But Hans Cobbler never expected to be remembered, and he was surprised that when he died, Roland came and carried him away to where the heroes live. There he lives still, and if you asked him now, "How goes it, Hans Cobbler?" he would answer, "Never better."

As for the land he won for Bremen, in time good houses were built there, and cows and horses grazed in green pastures. The bog was made into a park where children played, and the people took their pleasure on a little lake named for the Countess Emma, who outlived her nephew by many years. The story of Hans Cobbler was written on a stone bench that still stands by the lake in memory of his great day.

In the marketplace, an artist carved a great stone statue of Roland with his shield over his shoulder and his sword at his side. There he stands to this very day, guarding the freedom of Bremen. At his feet once upon a time was the likeness of Hans Cobbler. But time and weather took their toll. Even stone crumbles, and at last only the face of Hans was left, upturned at Roland's feet. It was usually children who noticed him.

Printed in the United States of America

First Edition

Library of Congress Cataloging-in-Publication Data
Hodges, Margaret.
The hero of Bremen / retold by Margaret Hodges ; illustrated by Charles Mikolaycak. — 1st ed.
p. cm.
Summary: Retells the German Legend in which a shoemaker who cannot walk helps the town of Bremen, aided by the spirit of the great hero Roland.
ISBN 0-8234-0934-1
[1. Folklore — Germany — Bremen.] I. Mikolaycak, Charles, ill. II. Title.
PZ8.1.H69He 1993 91-22357 CIP AC
398.2 — dc20
[E]

Design by Charles Mikolaycak

The illustrations in this book were prepared with watercolors on diazo prints made from pencil drawings. The text type was set in 14-point Goudy Sans Medium. The display type was set in Eckmann.

Thanks to Nicola and Elisabeth. C.M.

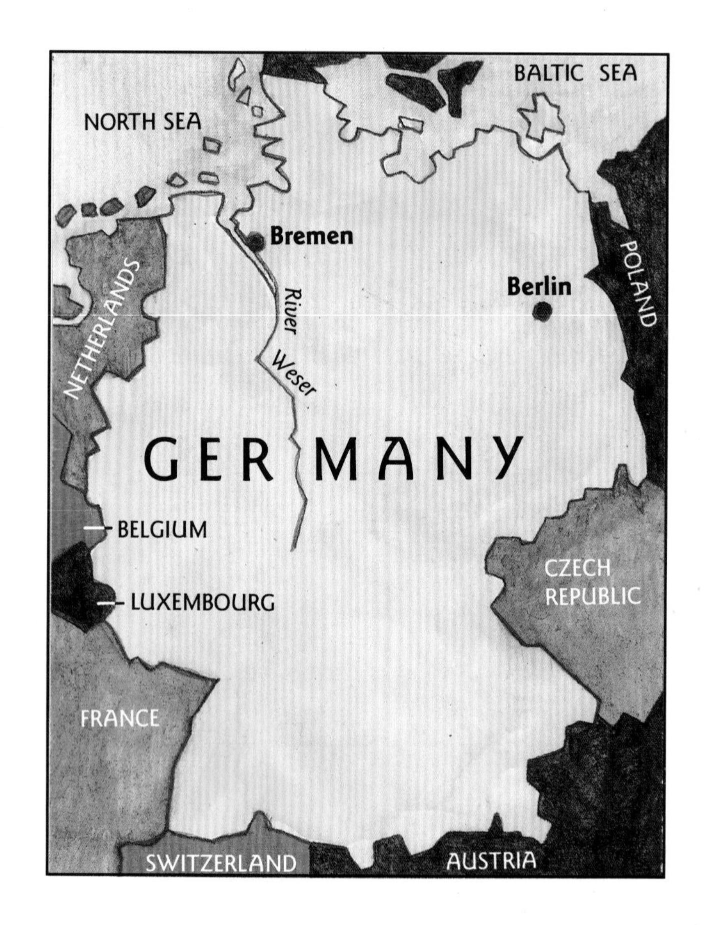